CHUCKIE
MAKES MISTAKES
(sometimes)

DEDICATION

This book is dedicated to all of Chuckie's loyal fans around the world (aka Team Chuckie).

I would also like to thank my husband Roger and our family and friends for being so supportive of my creative endeavors.

And a very special thank you goes to my collaborators Ulana Zahajkewycz and Amy Keller for helping to make this book become a reality!

Love,
Chuckie

Chuckie is a Chocolate Lab,
a handsome one indeed.

He always tries his very best,
but does not always succeed.

Chuckie makes mistakes
(sometimes).

Chuckie loves to dance,
Chuckie loves to play.

He loves to give kisses
(and he could do that all day!)

Chuckie does not
always realize when
he sits a little close.

He just wants to show
you that he cares, that
he loves you the most!

When Mommy and Daddy get home from work, Chuckie gets excited.

He needs to be the first one there, he's happy, he can't hide it!

Chuckie's favorite food to eat is lots of peanut butter. His sister Nestlé likes it too, (he can be a pesky little brother)!

Chuckie gets so happy when the mailman comes to call.

He jumps in the truck, eats the mailman's snack, and that's not polite at all!

Sometimes Chuckie sees his Mommy's sandals on the floor.

Even though he knows he shouldn't, they are too hard to ignore.

When Chuckie sees someone outside, his manners he forgets.

He shouts hello with his outside voice, and Daddy gets upset!

Chuckie likes to play around,
he likes to tease and chase.

But sometimes others don't
want to go at such a rapid pace.

Even though Chuckie makes mistakes, he has some good intentions.

He just forgets to be careful at times, and this can cause some tensions.

Every day, he will try,
to always do his best.

He will try to wait his turn,
to give his siblings a rest.

MAIL

He will try to say 'Excuse Me',
'Please' and 'Thank You' too.

He will ask if someone wants to play, instead of barrelling through!

He will try to ask before he takes,
to make sure he's allowed.

If he keeps all these good manners up,
he'll stand out from the crowd!

And yes it's true, he'll make mistakes, because nobody's perfect.

But using good manners and thinking of others shows caring and respect!

Chuckie Jensen

Chuckie the Chocolate Lab is an extremely handsome and sometimes mischievous dog who loves to be the center of attention.

——— YOU CAN FOLLOW CHUCKIE! ———

Facebook:
Chuckie the Chocolate Lab
#TeamChuckie

Instagram:
chuckie_the_chocolate_lab_

Left to right: Chuckie, Amy, Roger and Nestlé
Photo credit: KCW Photography

About the Author:
Amy Jensen

Amy Jensen is an author, playwright and teacher of Vocal Music at Warren Middle School in Warren Township, NJ. This is her first children's book and collaboration with Ulana Zahajkewycz. Amy has also co-written two shows with Landon Heimbach; a children's musical titled *"What's Your Favorite Color?"* and a comedy play titled *"Guess Who's Coming To Christmas"*. Amy received the Excellence in Education Recognition Award in 2012. She earned her Bachelor of Music Education degree from Westminster Choir College and her Master of Curriculum and Instruction degree from the American College of Education. She lives in Bridgewater, NJ with her husband Roger, their two chocolate labs, Chuckie and Nestlé, and their cat Bert.

About the Illustrator:
Ulana Zahajkewycz

Ulana Zahajkewycz is a freelance illustrator and an adjunct professor at Moore College of Art and Design in Philadelphia, PA. She is also the co-owner of the Carnival of Collectables Antique and Art Mall, in Sicklerville, NJ. Ulana exhibits her art nationally and her print, *"Murder She Wrote"* is part of the permanent collection at the Frederick R. Weisman Museum of Art in Minneapolis, MN. Ulana lives in New Jersey with her partner Brian and their adorable cat, Underdog.

Graphic Designer: Amy Keller Please visit www.coroflot.com/Akeller to view her portfolio.

Made in the USA
Monee, IL
20 December 2019